FrankinSchool

*TO FREDRIK—my son, who
got the wrong inscription that
started it all many years ago.*

FrankinSchool
Monster Match

by Caryn Rivadeneira
illustrated by Dani Jones

RED
CHAIR
·PRESS·

Egremont, Massachusetts

RED CHAIR PRESS
BOOKS FOR YOUNG READERS

www.redchairpress.com

Free Discussion Guide Available online

Publisher's Cataloging-In-Publication Data
(Provided by Cassidy Cataloging Services, Inc.)

Names: Rivadeneira, Caryn Dahlstrand, author. | Jones, Dani, 1983-
illustrator.

Title: Frankinschool. Monster match / by Caryn Rivadeneira ; illustrated by
Dani Jones..

Description: Egremont, Massachusetts : Red Chair Press, [2023] | Interest
age level: 007-010. | Summary: While Fred is out sick, a visiting author
signs Fred's book "To Frank". When Fred's desk-mate Luisa suggests Fred
must really be Frank in school, this sparks an idea for Fred's creative
writing assignment. Fred's What-If poem is coming together wonderfully,
until--a mist fills the room and the writing assignment comes to life.
Suddenly Fred--now Frankinschool--and Luisa--now Princessa Luisa--
need to save the school from the mysterious potion--and the even more
mysterious and devious ghost living in the school attic.--Publisher.

Identifiers: ISBN: 978-1-64371-241-3 (trade hardcover) | 978-1-64371-243-7
(multi-user ebook PDF S/L) | 978-1-64371-245-1 (ePub3 TR) | 978-1-
64371247-5 (audiobook) | LCCN: 2022940257

Subjects: LCSH: Creative writing--Juvenile fiction. | Monsters--Juvenile
fiction. | Ghosts--Juvenile fiction. | Friendship--Juvenile fiction. |
Schools--Juvenile fiction. | CYAC: Creative writing-- Fiction. | Monsters-
-Fiction. | Ghosts--Fiction. | Friendship--Fiction. | Schools-- Fiction.
| LCGFT: Ghost stories. | BISAC: JUVENILE FICTION / Books &
Libraries. | JUVENILE FICTION / Monsters. | JUVENILE FICTION /
Social Themes / Friendship.

Classification: LCC: PZ7.1.R57627 Fr 2023 | DDC: [Fic]--dc23

LC record available at https://lccn.loc.gov/2022940257
Main body text set in Amasis Regular 17/27
Text copyright © Caryn Rivadeneira
Copyright © 2024 Red Chair Press LLC

Printed in Canada

0523 1P F23FRN

TABLE OF CONTENTS

CHAPTER 1:

THE TROUBLE BEGINS

There once was a boy named Fred. Or, at least, he *thought* that was his name. He'd been Fred yesterday as he coughed and sneezed and shivered on the sofa. He'd been Fred when his mother drizzled his name in syrup across his pancake this morning, before he came back to school after being out sick.

And he'd been Fred as he waited in line on the playground, where friends welcomed him back and Luisa pestered him about where he'd been. "I bet you were faking, Fred," Luisa had said.

And he was still Fred as he slid into his desk that morning, sorting through the stack of worksheets he'd missed. In fact, he'd stayed Fred right up to the moment his teacher, Ms. Martinez, handed him a book and said, "Too bad you missed the author's visit yesterday." (*Had she used his name?* He couldn't remember.)

So it *had* to be Fred who smiled at the book, *Limbo Lessons*, with the picture of ruffle-shirted partygoers bending low under a limbo stick. Just like his aunt had at the family reunion last summer. (He shuddered at the memory.) It was definitely Fred who cracked open the book and whose eyes wandered to the words scribbled in black pen across the bright white page. The words, that is, that started all the trouble.

To Frank

"Frank?" Fred said to no one in particular. "Who's Frank?"

"What do you mean, *Who's Frank?*" Luisa said, leaning in close to see what Fred was looking at.

"I got somebody else's book by mistake," Fred said, pointing to the writing.

"Ahhh," Luisa said with a nod. "Thing is: there are no Franks at this school. None in the whole town, I bet! Maybe you wrote your name wrong on the order sheet. Like a dummy."

Fred rolled his eyes and shook his head. He'd watched his mom fill out the order form for the author visit. *Yes, my student would like a book.* She'd checked that box. Fred had seen her. And on the

line that read *Please inscribe the book to*
_____, he'd watched her
block the letters F-R-E-D. In case someone
didn't know how to spell Fred.

"Or, maybe it's something else," Luisa
said. "Like, maybe the author knows
something you don't."

"Like what?" Fred asked.

"Like, maybe you were *once* named
Fred," Luisa said. "But you aren't anymore.
Or, or, maybe you're still Fred at home, but
Frank in school."

"Frank in school?" Fred said. "Why
would I be that?"

"Kids?" Ms. Martinez snapped her
fingers at the boy once named Fred and
the girl still called Luisa. "Quiet please."

"See?" Luisa said. "Ms. Martinez didn't use your name."

"She didn't use yours either."

"Because she's not used to them. It hasn't sunk in that you're Frank in school and I'm *Princesa* Maria Luisa Octavia in school. Much fancier than dumb old Frank. That's for sure."

"Why's Frank dumb?"

"Because *you're* dumb. And *you're* Frank. In school."

Fred hung his head and huffed. He was done with Luisa's meanness. Every day she'd sat at the desk next to his and every day she'd said something awful to him. His mom said he should be honest: "Tell Luisa it bugs you. She'll stop."

But Fred didn't want Luisa to think he was dumb *and* a baby. The worst part was that his mom said that no matter what—even if Luisa kept being mean and didn't say she was sorry—he should *forgive* her. Fred never liked the sound of that. He thought something better was in order. Like seeing her trip up the stairs. That would teach her who the dummy was.

"Okay, everyone," Ms. Martinez said. "Creative writing time. Get your materials out."

The class groaned. Fred slid the open book to the back of his desk. He fished under his desk for a pencil and reached for his journal.

"No groaning, guys," Ms. Martinez said.

"It's going to be fun. Our prompt? 'What if' stories. Just ask yourself, *What if…?* Then, imagine and write. Be creative. Discover the power of pretend. Extra credit for rhymes."

Fred groaned alone this time. He hated rhymes. Now *they* were dumb. Besides, what on earth would he write about?

Luisa's pencil flew across her paper. She turned toward him and smirked.

Fred rolled his eyes. *What if Luisa tripped up the stairs?* How would that be as a story? Nah. Ms. Martinez wouldn't like that.

Fred slumped in his seat and looked at the ceiling for inspiration. Nothing. He turned to look out the window. Again, nothing. So he looked back to the book resting on his desk, to the words scratched out on its open pages. *To Frank.*

What if…?

Fred snatched his pencil and scooted his journal into a better position.

What if I am Frank in school? Fred wrote. He looked at the words: *Frank in school. Frank-in-school. Frankinschool!*

A smile spread across Fred's face. Frankinschool might not be fancy, but it sure might be fun. And so the boy once named Fred picked up his pencil and began to write.

What if I were Frankinschool?

I would not obey any rule.

I'd stomp and I'd snort,

I'd twist neck-screws for sport.

My lab would be in the attic of school!

That's the place you'd see me rule.

Creak open that door, sneak up those
    stairs

If I get caught, know what? Who cares!

I'd hide under the rafters

And shake with laughter

As I tamed the bats

And trained the cats

They'd sneak around the school at night

And gobble up any homework left in sight

From up in my attic I'd say what goes

I'd still learn stuff I'm supposed to know

I'd get to know ghosts who roam these
  halls

And see the critters that live in walls

I'd read about potions and work on my
  spells

Writing them down, so they'd go off during
  bells...

Fred paused, not sure what should

come next. Until he noticed Luisa shooting glances at his paper, before rolling her eyes and mouthing "looks dumb" at him.

Fred wrapped his arm across his paper, tucked his head down, and with a grin he added:

No Princesa Maria Luisa Octavias allowed, of course

She'd get carried away on her princessy horse...

The bell rang.

But as Ms. Martinez lifted her head to dismiss them to music class, a green mist crawled into the classroom. Fred stopped writing. His eyes lifted off the page he'd scribbled across to watch the fog's pillowy tendrils reach up desk legs and twist around students. Fred scanned the room, his mouth hanging open. One by one, the students' eyes closed and their heads drifted toward their desks, each one landing with a soft thud.

Luisa's head thudded harder. Fred wanted to laugh—normally he would have, served her right for calling him dumb—but then he saw Ms. Martinez crumple at the bookcase, her body bending and folding

neat as a dancer's.

Fred stood up, tried to race over, but his feet stuck to the ground. He looked down and gasped. Fred shot his hands out in front of him. They were as he suspected. He clutched his hands to his neck. Again, just as he thought.

Heavy-booted feet. A gray jacket, two sizes too small. Pea-green skin. A knobbed neck. The boy once named Fred was Fred no longer. He had become Frankinschool.

CHAPTER 2:

A MONSTER ON THE LOOSE

Frankinschool dragged heavy, booted feet across the carpeted classroom toward Ms. Martinez. He rested his wrinkled green fingers on the base of her neck, like he'd seen done in movies. Frankinschool wasn't quite sure what he was feeling for, but when a tha-thump, tha-thump, tha-thump rumbled below his fingers, he knew she was all right. Ms. Martinez was alive. As were his classmates. Frankinschool could see their shoulders rise and fall behind their heads settled on their desks. Frankinschool noticed drool dripping from the corner of Luisa's mouth. Again, Frankinschool would not laugh. But, he *would* tease her about it later.

At least, he hoped he would.

Frankinschool blinked twice, then three times more. He'd seen his mom do that when she tried not to cry. But as Frankinschool widened his eyes to keep the tears away, his forehead felt tighter than normal. He felt a crinkle.

Of course, Frankinschool thought as he raised his green fingers to explore his forehead. *Stitches*.

No amount of blinking or wide-eying could help now. As Frankinschool slumped into Ms. Martinez's wood-spindled chair, giant frankintears spilled out of his eyes, striping his green cheeks with wet gray.

"What are you crying about?" someone asked.

Frankinschool looked up.

Luisa. Or, someone like her.

"So now you're dumb *and* a baby?"

Frankinschool looked from the puddle of drool at her desk to the Luisa-like girl now standing beside it. She wiped her face with black-gloved hand. She straightened her riding jacket and dusted off her riding boots.

"I'm not a baby and I'm not dumb," Frankinschool said. "But who are you?"

"What do you mean?"

"You're not Luisa."

"Like you're not Fred," the Luisa-like girl said, as she raised her chin and shook her hair. "You're Frankinschool, and I, kind sir, am as I told you earlier: *Princesa Maria Luisa Octavia.* The first. You can call me

Princess. Pleasure to meet you."

"Princess?" Frankinschool said. "Where's your gown? Where's your *crown*?"

"Princesses don't *always* wear gowns—and rarely wear crowns. Especially when we want to ride horses."

Frankinshool looked around. He didn't see any horses, which was good. Horses made him nervous.

"But if you need proof of my princess-ness, here," Princess said. She walked toward Frankinschool and reached out her gloved hand and wriggled it. A circle of diamonds jiggled at her wrist.

Frankinschool nodded, took her hand, and shook it.

"*That's* not how you greet a princess," she

said. "You're supposed to *kiss* my hand."

"And *that's* not how you're supposed to meet a monster," Frankinschool said. "You're supposed to scream."

"But I'm not afraid," Princess said. "Okay, so no gowns, no crowns, no hand kissing and no screaming. But what are we going to do about all of *them*?"

"I don't know," said Frankinschool. "Go get help, I guess."

"Who's going to help us? That fog rolled in from the hallway—and who knows where else. Everyone else in town might be sleeping too," Princess said.

"So why aren't we?" Frankinschool asked.

"Well, I *was*. Until I felt something *wet*

under my cheek." Princess shuddered. "The *idea* that a princess would *drool* so appalled me that I woke up. Instantly."

Frankinschool smiled. Then he laughed. It felt good—even if it stretched his stitches.

"I don't think *you* should be laughing at anyone, knobby neck," Princess said. "If you're going to keep that up, you should thud back into your laboratory."

"My laboratory?" Frankinschool said. "Wait. That's it! My lab! That's where we need to go for help. Come on."

Frankinschool reached his green hand toward Princess's gloved one and pulled her toward the door. Plumes of puffy fog billowed up and down the staircase outside their door and rolled across the hallway.

They stepped into the fog toward Mrs. Jackson's class. Sure enough, every head rested on the desks in there, too.

"Over here," said Frankinschool, as he and Princess squinted their way through the fog, past Mr. Sanchez's room, past Ms. Blue's and toward yet another staircase. "This way."

"But there's nothing up there," Princess said. "Just the storage room."

"We're going to the attic," Frankinschool said. "It's through that door."

Frankinschool clomped up the stairs, steadying himself on the iron rail. He'd never been on this landing—not even to help take down goblins and spiders to decorate the Halloween Carnival, or to get the paper turkeys and pumpkins at Thanksgiving, or the tinsel and fake snow during Christmas.

But even though he'd never seen a janitor, principal, or even sneaky student creak open this secret door, he'd always known where it would lead.

The attic.

And he knew what he'd find up there. Just as he'd imagined. Just as he'd written during creative writing.

His laboratory.

That's where he and Princess would figure out what was going on.

CHAPTER 3:

THE BATS IN THE ATTIC

Frankinschool and Princess stared at the door.

"You think it's locked?" Princess said.

"Only one way to find out," Frankinschool said.

Frankinschool reached for the knob—dull and crusted with rust and chipped paint—and he turned it. Nothing.

"It's not moving," Frankinschool said.

"Let me try," said Princess.

Again, nothing.

Frankinschool bent down.

"There's something under that paint on the knob," Frankinschool said. "A design."

Frankinschool scratched at the knob with his rough nails.

"Gross!" Luisa said, as the paint flecks and rust flaked off the knob, revealing etchings in the doorknob. One line swirled to the right, then back to the left where it circled around itself again before swirling back to the right.

"It's like a locker combination," Frankinschool said. "I saw my sister practice her gym lock at home before school started. Two turns to the right, one to the left, and back to the right. But this is different. One to the right, then two to the left, and back right."

"But that makes no sense. Who's ever heard of opening a door that way?"

"None of this makes any sense," Frankinschool said. He held out his green arms, then pointed to the knobs on his neck. "None of this. So, let's just try."

Frankinschool reached for the handle. Slowly, he turned the knob to the right. Then to the left and left again. Then back to the right. They heard a click.

"Step back," Frankinschool said.

He pulled the door open.

They looked inside and then at each other. The thick sleeping fog had encircled their every step since leaving the classroom.

But it stopped—dead—at the doorway. It didn't—or couldn't—climb the flight of wooden stairs that stretched out ahead of them.

"That's weird," Princess said.

"Yeah," said Frankinschool, spinning around to check the status of the fog behind and below them. "Well, let's go up."

"After you, monster-sir," Princess said, stepping back.

Frankinschool nodded and gulped. Then he slid his boot forward, lifting his boot up slowly and landing it as soft as he could on the splintered first step.

"You're going to have to move faster than that," Princess said. "Everybody needs our help. And quick! Hyah!"

Frankinschool grabbed the railing and pulled himself up. Princess followed. One step, two steps, three steps, all the way up the rickety-crickety, wood-paneled

stairway that took them to the attic. They
gasped.

Under the roof, with its slanted eaves
and peeling rafters, were tables lined
with tiny steaming black cauldrons and

bubbling potions in beakers. Eyedroppers and glass stirrers, and measuring spoons and test tubes lay scattered in the few empty spaces between.

Books stacked in old wooden milk crates lined the walls. Above them, tiny black lumps hung from the rafters. Squeaks and

scratches drew their eyes to the nooks and corners, until—

"Look out!" said Princess.

Frankinschool bobbed his head down just in time to miss one of the tiny black lumps, now spread wide with thin velvety wings.

"A bat," said Frankinschool. He pointed to the ceiling and shuddered. "Make that bats. Plural."

Princess nodded. "And those are mice," she said, pointing to the nearest corner, where three tiny brown rodents tumbled over each other to get to a slice of bread, stiff and dry and smeared with remnants of grape jelly.

"Bats *and* mice...?" Frankinschool said, his mind drifting back. "This is starting to sound familiar... *As I tamed the bats and trained the cats they'd sneak around the school at night...*"

"Gobbling up everybody's homework, right?" said Princess, smiling at Frankinschool.

"Hey! You weren't supposed to be reading what I wrote."

"Well, I wasn't. Until I read something about me on a princessy horse. I liked the sound of that. Well, I *did*, until now."

Both looked back down the stairs to see the fog continuing to crash and roll over itself at the doorway.

"Yeah," said Frankinschool. "We need to find out what's going on. And how to stop it."

CHAPTER 4:

GHOSTS AND MONSTERS

Frankinschool walked up to one of the lab tables. He put his face close to a steaming cauldron and breathed in.

"I wouldn't do that!" said Princess.

"But we need to find out what's making this fog!"

"It's obviously not coming from here. The fog won't even come up the stairs."

"It's not rolling *out* from here," said Frankinschool. "But maybe someone took one of these beakers somewhere else. Maybe someone knew how to make it go *everywhere.*"

"But who would do that?" said Princess.

"Someone who wanted everyone to go to sleep, I guess," said Frankinschool.

"But this is *your* lab. Why would you invent something to make everyone go to sleep?"

"I don't know," said Frankinschool. And he didn't.

Sure, the boy once called Fred had laughed at the idea of Princess galloping away, of being banned from his attic lab, and maybe once about her tripping up those stairs. But he didn't want people to get *hurt.* Not actually. He just didn't want her to be so mean to him—or to call him dumb like she did.

"So who else knows about your lab?"

"*I didn't even know about my lab.* Not until I wrote it."

"Think back. To your poem. Who else is supposed to be up here? Besides the bats and the mice and the roaming cats. I know not me. *I'm* not allowed," said Princess.

Frankinschool's heart felt heavier than his boots as he looked at Princess's face. Her normally tight lips had relaxed into a tiny crooked smile and her normally glaring eyes looked at him softly. Frankinschool knew the look because he'd felt it. Princess Maria Luisa Octavia—no matter how fancy, no matter how mean—was hurt.

"Princess, it's not that—"

"No. I know. I know I say mean things. I know lots of people don't like me. But, you're so nice. I guess, I thought you knew I was teasing. I thought you liked me. I didn't know you didn't want me around."

"I don't *not* like you," Frankinschool said. "I don't like being called dumb. It bugs me. Even if you are teasing."

Princess hung her head. "I'm sorry," she said. "You're not dumb. I mean, dummies can't create all of this, can they?"

Princess threw her arms wide, meaning to point out what Frankinschool had created, but instead, she knocked over a bubbling beaker, sending shards of glass and an oozing liquid across the attic floor.

"Oh no!" she said.

Frankinschool stomped in a circle, looking around for a rag to clean up the spill.

"Look," said Princess. She crouched down closer to the bubbling gook.

Frankinschool yanked her arm back. "Don't touch it," he said.

"I won't," said Princess. "But this is weird. That looks like a shoe print!"

They both gasped as yet another print appeared in the gook. They held

their breath as another showed up, then another, and another. Their eyes drifted from the floor, up toward the ceiling as two of the bats zoomed in on something—or someone!—they couldn't see.

"It's the ghost," Frankinschool whispered.

"What ghost?" Princess whispered back.

"The ghost from the poem. That's who else is up here."

"No need to whisper," a voice said.

Frankinschool and Princess jumped.

"I can hear you—whether you whisper or shout. If I work really hard, I can even hear your thoughts. Hold on a sec..."

Frankinschool and Princess stood and took a slow step backward as an image of a man took shape right before their eyes.

Frankinschool turned, expecting to see an old school projector spinning out this movie of a man.

"Nope, I'm not a movie. I'm a real, honest-to-goodness ghost," the ghost said. "See? I can read your thoughts! Name's Frank."

Frank held his hand toward Frankinschool.

"*You're* Frank?" Frankinschool and Princess said together.

"In the flesh," Frank said. "Well, you know what I mean..."

Frankinschool stared at Frank, eyes wide and mouth open. Frankinschool didn't move a muscle until Princess nudged him.

"I'm, I'm—" Frankinschool started.

"He's Frank too, in a way," said Princess, jutting her hand in front of Frankinschool. "He's Frankinschool. And I, sir, am *Princesa* Maria Luisa Octavia."

Frank took Princess's hand and kissed it.

"*Enchanté, mademoiselle,*" Frank said.

Princess giggled, then turned to Frankinschool with a huff. "At least some people know how to greet a lady!"

"You're *not* a lady," said Frankinschool. "Just like he's not a person. He's a *ghost.*"

"Well," said Frank. "I'm the spirit of a person. That should count for something."

"I guess so," said Frankinschool. "But, who are you? I mean, who *were* you?"

Frank laughed. "The best thing about having—and being—a spirit is that you're still the same person whether you've got a body or not."

"But if you don't have a body," Princess said, "how'd you make those prints in the gook?"

Frank laughed again. "You're good, Princess. You'd make a fine detective."

Princess beamed. Frankinschool rolled his eyes.

"So how *did* you make them?" Frankinschool asked.

"I didn't," said Frank. "Those are *your* prints, from before. My feet aren't that big!"

Frankinschool looked down at his huge boots.

"That potion simply reveals footprints one at a time," Frank said. "Creepy, isn't it?"

Princess nodded.

"So, when you knocked over the potion and the prints showed up, I just hovered over them as they appeared," said Frank.

"It worked out well, though. I wasn't sure how I was going to reveal myself to you guys. I'm glad you figured out the doorknob. Opening a door yourself is less scary than having it creak open on its own. If you got *too* scared, I was afraid you might not come up."

"Why would you want us to come up?" Frankinschool asked.

"I didn't mean for you to come up, not originally. I wanted you guys to fall asleep like everyone else. But that was a new sleeping potion. I hadn't used that one before. I'm still not sure why it didn't work on you two. Or, why you got green and knobby and why you got fancy. You two must have something powerful going on in those noggins."

"But why did you want everyone to fall asleep?" Princess asked.

"I needed to grab my book, didn't I?"

"But that's not *your* book," Frankinschool said. "It's mine. I'm Frankinschool. The book even says so."

"No," said Frank. "You're Frankinschool because *you* wrote that. The book says *To Frank* because it's *to* me. It's my book. I got a copy like everyone else. I always do when authors visit." Frank motioned to the walls lined with books. "Only so many times I can read these same books."

"How do you buy a copy?" Princess asked. "Ghosts don't have money."

"Nope," Frank said. "We don't. But all it

takes is one little whisper in the author's ear while she's signing books and *voila!* I get my own signed copy."

"But you got a book that was supposed to be mine! My mom paid for it. It should've said To Fred."

"Happens to one kid every time," Frank said. "I can't believe no one's noticed before. The trick of it has always been figuring out how to get the book up here. Sometimes I sneak in at recess, but that's boring. These sleeping potions I've been working on are much more fun."

"So, this is what you do in my lab?" said Frankinschool. "Invent potions so you can steal stuff?"

"Oh, it's *your* lab now, huh?" Frank said. "You may have thought of it, but I'm the one up here using it. What do they say? Possession is nine-tenths of the law? Sorry, kid. *My* lab."

Frankinschool groaned. "Second thing you've taken from me. That's not fair."

"Kiddo, it *is* fair. I cleaned this school from top to bottom, scraped gum from under lunch tables, wiped pee off urinals and puke off desks for forty years—and somehow I end up spending spirit time in this same place? *That's* not fair. The least I can do is make potions in a lab to help me swipe a book every now and again."

"That does sound reasonable," Princess said.

Frankinschool glared at Princess. He wanted to tell her to shut up but suspected she'd tattle on him the moment Ms. Martinez woke up.

"So how about it, kids? Should we go get that book?"

Princess started for the stairs, but

Frankinschool grabbed her arm to stop her.

"No," Frankinschool said, pointing a long frankinnail at Frank. "My mother bought me that book with her hard-earned money. Just because you can whisper a name into an author's ear doesn't mean you can just steal things. That book is mine."

"It's got my name in it," Frank said. "You may be Frank in school but you're still Fred everywhere else."

"Maybe," Frankinschool said. "But whoever I am, *I* didn't turn green and grow knobs and watch my teacher's head conk on her desk and clomp through a foggy hallway just to give you my book.

I'm Frank now too. In school. That's my book."

Frank laughed. "Well, looks like I'll just have to go get it myself. Race you."

And with that, Frank disappeared through the floor.

Frankinschool turned toward the stairs.

"Our classroom is just below here," Frankinschool said. "We better be quick."

Now it was Princess's turn to stop Frankinschool from heading down the stairs.

"Wait," she said. "I have an idea."

Princess rushed over to a bookshelf and began grabbing books, reading titles off their spines and then throwing them to the floor. They landed in huge clouds of dust.

"Frank learned how to make the sleeping

potions from these books," Princess said. "There's got to be something in here to teach us how to set him free?"

"Set him free?" Frankinschool asked. "He should go to jail!"

"Jail?" Princess said. "Don't be silly. We need to help him."

"We came up here to help Ms. Martinez—and everyone downstairs!"

"But if we help him, we help everyone," Princess said. "This won't keep happening. Don't you get it? He's trapped here, so he's doing naughty things. If he were *free*, he'd stop stealing. We'd all stay awake. You'd go back to being Fred and I'd be Luisa again. Though—" Luisa jingled the diamonds on her wrists—"I really will miss these."

Frankinschool shook his head, but said, "Okay. What do we need to do to help him?"

"A potion... or a spell... or a... Wait. I got it!" Princess thrust a book at Frankinschool. Beneath the dust, Frankinschool barely made out the gold letters stamped across the battered green leather: *Time in Limbo*.

"Limbo?" Frankinschool asked.

"Yes, Limbo," Princess said.

"The thing you do under a stick?" Frankinschool asked.

"No, silly," Princess said. "The place you go to wait."

"Wait for what?" Frankinschool asked.

Princess flipped frantically through the pages, smiling when she settled on what she'd been looking for.

"As you wait for Heaven or..." Princess looked around before whispering. "The *other* place. Ugh. Haven't you ever been to church?"

"Of course I have. But I've never heard anyone talk about *limbo*."

"That's because not everyone believes in it," Princess said.

"People don't believe in ghosts either," Frankinschool said.

"Exactly," said Princess. "But here's the thing. People say ghosts aren't real and that limbo isn't real. And yet, here we are with Frank the Ghost. And he's in *limbo*. That's why he can't leave. He's in the waiting place. He's, he's..."

"Frankinlimbo," they said together.

Princess giggled.

"He is! He's Frankinlimbo," Princess said. "I don't know how to explain any of this. Except it's where your *what if* question got us. Limbo and ghosts *may* or may not be imaginary, but Frank still needs our help. And imaginary or not, we need to help him. There's a reason he's waiting here—maybe to learn? Maybe to teach? Maybe this book will show us what."

"Of course!" Frankinschool threw his hands up, startling the bat that had snuggled in above him. "The book! That's it. Except, it's not *that* book that's going to help us. We need *Limbo Lessons*. That's what this is all about."

"You need to learn how to do the limbo?" Princess asked.

"No. But just like I wrote in my poem: I need to learn something. Frank is my lesson. And if my *what if* question got us here, we're going to need a new *what if* question to get us out. I'm gonna need to write a new poem."

CHAPTER 5:

FRANK MEETS HIS MATCH

Frankinschool felt a thud under his feet. Then another. And another. A book—*his book*, *Limbo Lessons*—shot up through the floorboards. Frankinschool jumped out of the way, grabbing up the paper and pencil as he stood. Princess ducked from getting hit as it sailed to a table.

"Sorry about that," Frank said, wafting up through a small crack in the floor. "Took a few special tricks to get that book to pop up. Can't carry it, you see…"

"Then how do you flip pages?" Princess asked.

Frank bent toward the book and blew. Princess and Frankinschool shuddered at the chill. "Spirit breath is a handy thing."

"So you like being a spirit?" Frankin-school asked.

"I like being a spirit all right. I don't love being up here. Gets lonely."

"So, what if we found a way to free you?" Princess asked.

Frank laughed and pointed to *Time in Limbo* on the floor beside him. "I see you've been making good use of my library. You found good old *Time in Limbo* on my shelves. Now maybe you understand why I was so excited the author of *Limbo Lessons* was coming to this school. Limbo is a special interest of mine. But that book was much harder to get. I had to hoof it up to the *public* library for that one. Then I had to tangle with a couple of library ghosts to get it sent here. Library ghosts are the worst. Talk about scary!"

Frank cackled until he coughed. "But if you think *Time in Limbo* will free me, think again," Frank said. "It told me that most people think good deeds would get them out of limbo. So, I tried that. Believe me. It doesn't work. I spent my first decade here blowing crumbs off the floors, scaring the mice out of classrooms. I scared bullies and helped the kids nobody picked in gym class make amazing catches and touchdowns. I even managed to pull the fire alarm once when I smelled smoke in the boiler room. And... *nada*. Still here. So, I figure: if I was going to spend eternity in this place, I might as well have some fun."

"Well, I'm glad you've had 'fun,' but you should've turned the page," Princess said. She reached for the book, flipped the page, and began reading. "'Limbo isn't a physical, actual place. Spirits and ghosts don't lurk there. Instead, limbo is *wherever* we wait. Limbo is *whenever* we get stuck in between. In limbo, we wait and listen and learn.'"

Princess smacked the book shut with a huff and put it back on the table.

"And that's supposed to be good news?" Frank said. "What does all that gobble-dy-talk even mean?"

"It means," Frankinschool said, "we have a question for you: What if you aren't a ghost at all? What if you're not a ghost at all, but a phantom—a figment of my imagination? What if you're a lesson? What if you're *my* lesson?"

Frank laughed. "You kidding me? You think I'm not real? Like, I'm your *conscience* or something? You think I'm a *lesson*?"

Frankinschool nodded. "Well, Ms. Martinez said there's power in pretending. And clearly, there is. I'm not *really* a monster. She's not *really* a princess—"

"Well," Princess interrupted. "Actually, I kinda am."

"No," said Frankinschool. "You're not. And those aren't *really* bats and those aren't really mice and—wait? Weren't there supposed to be cats? Anyway, this isn't a real lab. This isn't real—not actual physical real anyway. It's make-believe. It's play-pretend. But just because it's imaginary doesn't mean it's not true—or that it can't teach us. Like Ms. Martinez said, our imaginations are powerful. And I think I know what I'm supposed to learn. Hold on."

Frankinschool rushed to a bookshelf and grabbed a sheet of paper out of an old recycling bin. He rustled around the lab tables until he found a pen. Frankinschool bent over a table and scribbled and scratched.

"Frank," Frankinschool said, straightening the sheet of paper. "I have a new poem for you. Ahem..."

What if Frank were not a ghost?
What if he were a phantom at most?
Then perhaps I would learn
What my mom hoped I'd discern
About forgiveness and mercy and toast

"And *toast*?" Princess said.

"Shush," Frankinschool said. "I was in a hurry and I needed a rhyme! Hold on.

There's more."

So I forgive you for stealing my book
I'll no longer think of you as a crook
I once learned about grace
When the bad things erase
And with that you're off the hook

Princess tilted her head toward Frank and said, "Corny, but true."

"I didn't have a lot of time to write this!" Frankinschool said. "I'm trying to hurry. Frank's been waiting a long time and people are still asleep downstairs, you know."

"Fair enough," said Princess.

"It wasn't a bad poem," said Frank.

Frankinschool sighed. "If it's good or

bad isn't the *point*," he said, grabbing his book off the table. He flipped open to the page dedicated *To Frank*.

"This book *is* mine," Frankinschool said. "Cheating your way to get it doesn't make it yours. No more than fighting off library ghosts makes those books yours. But the book will be yours if I give it to you. So, here. I want you to have it. I forgive you for taking it—and I get why you wanted it. But now, it really is *To Frank*. Free and clear."

Frankinschool handed the book to Frank. It fell to the floor.

"I can't hold it, kiddo," Frank said.

"Sorry," Frankinschool said, with a laugh. "You need one of your potions?"

Frank nodded and drifted over to the lab table and blew on a small beaker. A blue mixture poured out of it. Frank blew that into a large cauldron. Then he blew in a few shakes of a powder from a tiny nearby tub.

"This ought to do it," Frank said, as the potion spilled onto the floor, covering the book. And at that, the book's shiny jacket faded. They could see through it. It had become a ghost of a book.

Frank picked it up and held it to his ghost chest.

"Thank you," he said. "It's been a long time since I got a gift."

"You're welcome," said Frankinschool. "I hope you like it."

"I actually started it yesterday," said Princess. "It's not that good. The author was overrated."

They laughed. But Frank and the now ghost-book began to fade into the attic air. Frankinschool and Princess stepped forward to hug him but their arms sailed right through him.

A wet drop fell to the floor beneath

where Frank floated. Frankinschool and Princess looked at Frank's face. A steady stream spilled from behind his spirit eyes.

"How on Earth?" Princess asked.

"It's a drool potion," Frank said and pointed to a beaker that spit water high into the air. "It's set to release spit drool to

wake everybody up."

"Eww," said Princess. "Why drool?"

"Just for fun," Frank said. "And drool is always funny, right Frankinschool?"

Frankinschool smiled as Frank's form thinned into the air. "Now go back to your desks before everyone wakes up and wonders where you ran off to," they heard him say. "And your lesson isn't over. I'm not the only one who needed grace…"

The bats swirled and dived as Frank's image sparked and disappeared. He was gone.

Frankinschool looked at Princess. She was crying. No potions this time. Just real tears.

"I'm gonna miss Frank," she said.

"Me too," Frankinschool sniffed. His throat caught as he said, "But Frank was right. We better get back to the classroom. But one thing first. I have a poem for you too."

Princess raised an eyebrow. "*Okay*," she said.

Frankinschool turned the sheet of paper over and shook it before starting:

What if Princess Maria Luisa Octavia
   became my friend?

Then how might all this end?

I used to think that you were mean

But now I know there was more to be seen

You thought you were being funny

Now I hope you'll be a little more sunny

Because I'd like to be friends, you seem real
   nice

But we better go because I see some mice

"That's a weird ending," Princess said.

"But it's true," Frankinschool said.
"There are mice climbing the wall behind
you."

Princess turned and jumped at the sight.
"Yes, let's get out of here. But first,"

Princess said. "Frankinfriends?"

Frankinschool smiled and held out an upturned palm. Princess put hers in it and he fake-kissed it.

"Frankinfriends forever," he said.

"But until then, we better get back."

They gave the attic one last look.

"It sure does *look* real up here," said Princess.

"It's real enough," Frankinschool said. "We won't forget it."

A blob of drool dropped on Frankinschool's head and rolled down his cheek. Princess giggled and reached to wipe it off.

"Don't," Frankinschool said. "We need this wake-up drool to work on us. I don't want to stay Frankinschool forever."

"It'll work," said Princess.

"How do you know?" Frankinschool asked.

"Because you'll imagine a way it will," she said. "You're smart like that."

Princess galloped and Frankinschool clomped down the slatted stairs they'd only first climbed a short while ago. As they turned the corner to descend the short flight to their hallway, Princess tripped. Frankinschool caught her arm and steadied her.

"Careful," he said.

As they walked, the once-thick fog rolled away from them before breaking up into the hallway air. They paused for a moment as they watched it disappear.

"Reminds me of Frank," Frankinschool said.

"Yeah," Princess said. "I bet lots of things will."

They could hear teachers and kids from other classes chattering, scooting chairs back, and digging through desks, slamming closets like nothing had happened.

Frankinschool clomped faster. He and Princess reached their classroom door just as the students and Ms. Martinez were beginning to rouse. They slid into their chairs.

"All right, class," Ms. Martinez was saying. "That's the bell. Put your things away and get ready for Music."

But Frankinschool heard none of it. He didn't respond until he felt Ms. Martinez's hand on his back. He turned toward her. She looked worried. The potion must not have worked.

"Are you feeling sick again? Need to go to the nurse?" Ms. Martinez asked. "Looks like you've seen a ghost."

Ms. Martinez's eyebrows scrunched as

she moved her hand to his forehead.

Frankinschool shot his hands in front of him. No longer green. He reached for his neck. No more knobs. He looked at his feet. Regular old sneakers.

"Nah, I'm okay," Fred said. "Just tired, I guess."

"Tired and *dumb*," Luisa said.

Luisa winked but Fred didn't notice. He tossed his head back and rolled his eyes. *What a stupid dream. Like she could ever be nice. Like they could be friends. She was still the same old Luisa. Still,* he thought, *Mom was right. He should forgive her.* Fred sighed. He'd try.

Fred put his pencil and journal away. He stood up and stretched.

What a weird thing to dream about. Princesses. And ghosts. And attics. And limbo. And lessons. And gifts for invisible book-thieves. But still, it was good while it lasted.

Fred reached for the book still open on his desk. But as he went to close it, he noticed fresh writing, new scratches blurred at the edges, smudged with a green goo and a blue powder.

Fred gasped.

"I know, right?" Luisa whispered.

Fred jumped. He hadn't noticed her move around the desks.

"Frank's the best," she said. "Hope he likes being free from your imaginary limbo."

"Wait," Fred said. "You know Frank?"

"Of course I do, dummy—I mean, *smartie*," Luisa said.

"But, I dreamt all that. Or imagined it. It was just pretend."

"Yeah, well. Like Ms. Martinez said: The power of pretend and all that. Thanks for bringing me along," Luisa said, galloping toward the stairs and waving toward Fred. As she did, a circle of diamonds jiggled at her wrist. "Let's do it again sometime, Frank."

The Boy Once Named Fred and Then Named Frankinschool and Now Maybe Sometimes Frank smiled.

"Definitely," he said. "And, be careful on those stairs, Princess."

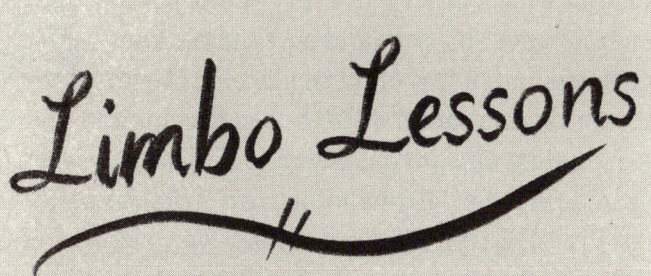

Limbo Lessons

To Frankinschool, er, Fred:

Thanks for the book—and the poem. Guess you weren't the only one who needed Limbo Lessons. I'm sorry I took this. It is yours and you should have it. Plus, Princess was right. It's overrated. Kidding. Hope you enjoy it. Pretend-visit me again some time.

Your friend,
—Frank